# Tl
## #1 Th

By Sara Lords

Illustrations by Staci Britton

2020

Anna & Emily -

This is a young friend I used to work with at Sare Staple. This is a fictional book with parts of their lives in it.

Enjoy
love
Nana

# About the Author

Sara Lords is the author of the Sister Wars Book Series and The Sister Wars Blog. She is based out of Portland, Oregon where she resides with her husband, daughter, and two stepchildren. Sara graduated from the University of Oregon and is certified in healthcare quality improvement. She works as a hospital Healthcare Quality Consultant while maintaining her love for writing and exploring the unique lives of blended families. Her own blended family is her greatest inspiration.

The Sister Wars

Copyright © 2020 Sara Lords LLC

All rights reserved. No part of this book may be used or reproduced in any manner whatsoever without written permission except in the case of brief quotations embodied in critical articles and reviews.

This book is a work of fiction. Any reference to historical events, real people, or real places are used fictitiously. Other names, characters, places and incidents are the product of the author's imagination, and any resemblance to actual events, places or persons, living or dead, is entirely coincidental.

Written by Sara Lords
Illustrations by Staci Britton

Dedicated to the loves of my life;

Skye

Drew

Avy

Kavan

# **Contents**

| | | |
|---|---|---|
| Chapter One | .................... | **1** |
| Chapter Two | .................... | **11** |
| Chapter Three | .................... | **19** |
| Chapter Four | .................... | **32** |
| Chapter Five | .................... | **40** |
| Chapter Six | .................... | **51** |
| Chapter Seven | .................... | **62** |
| Chapter Eight | .................... | **74** |
| Chapter Nine | .................... | **82** |
| Chapter Ten | .................... | **93** |

# Chapter One

I stare at my digital clock, willing the minutes to go by faster. I close my eyes for what feels like an eternity, then slowly let them flutter open. Nope, the clock still reads 4:57. What's taking them so long? Olivia and Alex were supposed to be home from their mom's house twenty-seven minutes ago. I've been home from my dad's for hours and the house feels empty without my stepsister and stepbrother.

My parents divorced around my second birthday. I don't remember them together at all.

It makes me sad sometimes, but I know my mom is happy now. On the plus side, I get two houses, two Christmases, and two birthdays every year. I see my dad, Matthew, a few nights a week. Olivia and Alex see their mom, Kimberly, a few nights a week too. It's a little weird to only see your sister and brother four nights a week, but Mom said a lot of families are like ours now. Lots of parents get divorced. Lots of kids have stepmoms and stepdads. Lots of kids have stepsisters and stepbrothers. Lots of kids go back and forth.

The front door finally chimes, and I jump up and run downstairs at the sound of our dog, Chase, barking a greeting to Olivia and Alex.

Before I can even see them, I shout, "Olivia! I'm so glad you're home. Guess who I saw when I was with my dad?" I'd been holding in the news and felt like I was going to burst. If anyone was going to appreciate this gossip, it was Olivia. When I'd been out to dinner with my dad last night, I'd seen our music teacher at the restaurant. This normally wouldn't be that exciting except she was with Caleb Prescott and his dad. Caleb is a boy in our class and there had been rumors his dad was dating our music teacher.

I come to a stop in front of Olivia, but she just hangs up her coat without saying anything. "Olivia, did you hear what I said?"

"Oh, hi Jade. Yeah, I heard you." She puts her shoes away, then runs up the stairs to her room without another word. As I stand in the front entryway, unsure whether to follow or not, I hear the sound of her door closing upstairs. What was that about? Olivia is usually so excited to see me and catch up after we've been away at our other parent's houses.

"Girls, hurry up. You're going to be late for cheer practice!" Mom's voice echoes through the house. With a shrug, I head up to my room to change. I don't have time to figure it out right now. I rummage through my closet, looking for my cheer outfit and hoping I didn't leave it at my dad's house. I won't be back at my dad's for a few days and I don't have a spare.

Luckily I find it buried under some clothes at the bottom of my dresser. I change as fast as I can, grab a jacket, and rush out of the house to join my mom and Olivia, who are waiting for me in the car. Olivia doesn't turn to chat with me like we normally would on a typical drive to practice. Instead, she's staring out her window and chewing on her bottom lip. Maybe she's nervous about our first cheer competition next week? I turn my attention to the rain splashing on the window and my mind drifts to the events of the past year.

I'd always dreamed of having a sister. When Olivia's dad, Ben, and my mom got married, my dream became a reality, and as a bonus, I now have a cool brother too.

But sometimes it's hard to face the truth. Olivia and I used to be best friends. We met for the first time about two years ago. Her dad had come over for dinner a few times to my mom's house, and I was slowly getting to know him. He seemed like a nice enough guy, but it was weird to have a man sitting at the dinner table that wasn't my dad.

    A few weeks after I met Ben, my mom told me I was going to meet his daughter, Olivia. He had already shown me a picture of Alex and Olivia on his phone. The three of them had been at a school carnival, and it looked like they were laughing and having a great time. Olivia looked sweet in the photo and Alex looked like how I imagined a tough older brother would look. I was nervous to meet them, but my mom told me Alex would be at a friend's birthday party. I was kind of relieved it would be just us girls and Ben.

    It was toward the end of the school year and the weather had warmed up enough to wear shorts. It had rained the day before so I had to be careful to avoid the muddy puddles in the driveway when I got in the car. I like muddy puddles but I hate the rain, which is unfortunate when you live in Seattle. When the weather is nice, I like to be outside as much as I can. I think it's why I suggested we meet Olivia and her dad at the park that day. It might have also had something to do with my nerves. If I didn't like Olivia, or worse if she didn't like me, at least I could enjoy the park.

On the drive over, I mentioned being anxious to my mom. She always knows what to say to make me feel better. "What if Olivia doesn't like me?" I asked.

My mom pulled up to a red light and turned to look at me in the backseat. She smiled and said, "I'm sure you'll both like each other, you have a lot in common." She said Olivia and I were the same age and we both loved to dance and draw. She also said Olivia was super sweet, thoughtful, and funny.

By the time we had pulled up to the park, I couldn't get my seatbelt off fast enough. I jumped out of the car with the two jump ropes I'd brought with me. As soon as I spotted Ben talking with Olivia, I ran toward them.

"Olivia, you remember Sophie," Ben said as he put one arm around Olivia, who looked as nervous as I felt. "This is her daughter, Jade Parker."

Olivia's eyes lit up when she saw the jump ropes in my hand. "I love to jump rope! I'm on the jump rope team at school."

"You are? That's so cool. I wish we had a team at my school." I handed her one of the jump ropes and we spent the rest of the afternoon showing each other the tricks we knew and competing to see who could jump the most times without hitting the rope. We were instant best friends.

It wasn't long before we wanted to do everything together. My mom had been right about Olivia and I having a lot in common. We're both ten years old (we were eight back then). We both have British grandparents. We both love to draw and dance. We can spend hours watching dance competitions on tv. When our parents were dating, we spent a lot of time together, but we missed each other on the days we were with our other parents. We looked forward to the occasional sleep over. We would stay up all night whispering and sharing secrets. We talked about divorce, we talked about our parents, and we talked about the boys we liked at school.

We also both love to make up cheerleading routines. We had so much fun cheering together in her dad's living room those first few months, we begged our parents to sign us up for Blaze, a local competitive cheer squad. They agreed on two conditions: we would have to stick with the team for the season, and we would have to keep our grades up. The cheerleading squad was expensive and would take up a lot of time.

Olivia and I were willing to agree to anything to be on the team. We didn't realize how many hours a week it would be between the tumbling classes and cheer practices, but we loved it and we've stuck with it for over a year. When Coach Meyer announced two months ago that we were going to have our first cheer competition, I wasn't prepared for how nervous I would feel to compete.

We pull up to the gym and I shake my head and try to focus on the present. I sneak a glance at Olivia as we get out of the car. Her face is sullen. It has to be because of the cheer competition next week. What else would explain why she was being so distant?

# Chapter Two

"Girls, you're late." Coach Meyer claps her hands and ushers us toward the other girls when we finally make our way into the gym.

Olivia and I tell her we're sorry and begin warming up. My thoughts start to drift as I stretch, but I force myself to focus. The competition is next week, and I don't want to mess up our chances at winning our first trophy.

Throughout practice, I can't help but watch Olivia though. I just don't understand what's going on. Normally we warm up next to each other, but she went as far from me as she could be in the gym without leaving the group.

"Jade, you've got to pay attention." Coach Meyer states as I miss my cue to step forward for the basket toss portion of our routine.

"Sorry." I shake my head, but I don't think it's helping shake the thoughts away. I need to focus. I don't want to mess up during the competition so I need to get these steps down. Olivia and I are next to each other for the majority of the routine. We're supposed to give each other enough space to perform the back handspring but Olivia keeps stepping into my section of the mat. I try to compensate by moving over slightly. This causes me to land my back handspring out of formation and Coach Meyer asks that we try again.

"Can you please stop moving into my space?" I ask Olivia as we take our positions.

"I'm not moving into your space. It's not my fault if you don't know how to do a back handspring." Olivia huffs as she takes her position.

My mouth drops in shock. Olivia and I have been fighting a lot lately and I can't quite figure out why. I'd like to go back to the time when Olivia and I were excited to officially be sisters. My mom and Ben were married a few months ago. The actual wedding was amazing. Everyone had been so happy, and the day went by in a blur. I wish I could have hit pause. Olivia and I were so excited the night before the wedding we had a hard time falling asleep — we couldn't wait to wear the bridesmaid dresses my mom let us pick out and get our hair and makeup done. It felt like a fairytale. Sometimes I close my eyes and pretend it's still the wedding day.

It wasn't long after our parents were married when we started to notice our differences. I'm three months older than Olivia. She can spend all day drawing and sometimes I need to take a break to do cartwheels and flips. I like basketball but Olivia would rather watch from the side lines. I like to run outside, but Olivia likes to go on walks. I like to read for fun, but Olivia only reads when it's an assignment for school. I like to play the piano and Olivia likes to sing. I like my bedroom door open and Olivia likes hers shut.

Olivia is also more British than I am. Both of Ben's parents are British but one of my grandmothers is Persian. I've been told this makes me a quarter Persian. It seems to be a big deal to a lot of people but I like having tan skin and speaking a secret language with my mom.

The differences had always been there, but for some reason, they hadn't bothered us. When we were best friends, we were just happy to be spending time together. Everything changed when we became family. Everything changed when we became sisters. And it just seems to be getting worse and worse.

I have to shrug this off until later. I can't mess up again. Coach Meyer motions for us to start. I run down the mat and perform two forward flips, followed by a toe touch. It's then time for the back handspring. I take a deep breath and propel backward for the back handspring. My hand makes contact with the floor, but I'm struck by a pair of legs and I go tumbling down to the ground.

"Watch where you're going!" Olivia yells as she jumps up and moves her legs away from me.

"Watch where I'm going? You're the one that ran into me!" I yell at her in disbelief. I can't believe she's blaming me for her mistake.

"Girls, that's enough, please get back in your positions and make sure you're staying in your space," said Coach Meyer. Olivia and I glare at each other as we take our spots. We manage to get through the back handspring without any more collisions. Coach Meyer blows her whistle and practice is over. I run to the sideline to grab my water bottle and as I turn to walk out of the gym, I'm startled when Olivia rams her shoulder into mine.

"Hey! What was that for?" I rub my shoulder and stare down at her as she crouches to grab her water bottle.

"What was what for? You need to pay attention and stop running into me." She stands up and exits the gym. It takes me a minute to process what transpired. The blood rushes to my head and my face grows hot. I run out the gym, and as Olivia is getting into my mom's car, I grab her arm and swing her around to face me.

"Don't touch me," she screams. Our faces are only inches apart.

I place my hands on my hips and square my shoulders, "What's your problem?" I ask.

Before she can answer, Mom rolls her window down. "Girls, that's enough, get in the car." I walk over to my side of the car but my eyes never leave Olivia's. Mom asks us for an explanation once we're settled in the car but Olivia and I refuse to answer. We drive home in silence and I seethe with anger and a hurt deep in my chest. I don't care if she's nervous about the competition anymore. She really hurt my feelings. We're supposed to be sisters. We're supposed to be best friends. Olivia and I run up to our rooms as soon as we get home and the hurt in my chest expands.

# Chapter Three

"Jade, can you please come downstairs?"

"Yes, Mom." I tuck my long black hair behind my ears and out of my green eyes, hoping that she doesn't want to talk about the fight Olivia and I had earlier after dance class. The last time, she gave me a long speech about how we were sisters now and we had to be nice to each other. And we definitely weren't doing that right now. Maybe she just needs help setting the table? Maybe if I show her how sorry I am, she might spare me a lecture? With a sigh, I turn toward the stairs and take my time walking down to the kitchen.

"What on earth is going on with you and Olivia?" Mom faces the stove as she places grilled chicken onto the serving platter.

I wait for her to turn around, but she grabs a spoon and starts to scoop the mashed potatoes into a bowl. I better answer her or I'm going to be in real trouble. I tug at the bottom of my black t-shirt and stare at the floor, trying to come up with a good excuse for all of the yelling. When she turns to face me, I still have nothing clever to say. Her eyes dim with disappointment.

"I thought we talked about this. Walk away and give yourselves some space to calm down." Mom pulls her hair into a ponytail and rolls her neck back and forth. I want to tell her how mad I am at Olivia. I want to tell her I wish we could go back in time to when it was just me and her. I want to tell her I miss my old life, but she hates to cook and she was home late from work today. She's not going to be in the mood.

Shaking her head, she says, "I don't understand why you two are acting like this. You used to love spending time together."

I know I need to talk to her about what's going on, but with dinner almost ready, now's not the best time. Instead, I give her a quick kiss on the cheek, say, "Sorry, Mom, I love you," and turn to leave the kitchen.

Before I can make my exit, "I really want to talk to you about this more," mom said.

"I know mom but can we talk when we have more time?" I hold my breath in anticipation of her response.

Mom pauses as she sets the platter of chicken onto the dinner table, "Sure, dinner is almost ready why don't you set the table?" A wave of relief washes over me. A real conversation will have to wait for when I can say everything I need to say. I set the table and mom calls the rest of the family downstairs for dinner.

"Can you pass the potatoes please?"

I pick up the bowl of mashed potatoes and pass them to Alex. He scoops a big spoonful onto his plate, then clears his throat several times as he places them back on the table. I watch as he gets up off his chair, crouches down, and wipes the floor several times with his hands. His shaggy brown hair falls over his eyes as he touches the sides of the table. He sits back on his chair and resumes eating. My mom and stepdad share a concerned look with each other.

Alex has O.C.D., short for Obsessive Compulsive Disorder. My family calls it "habits." He repeats things a lot, like clearing his throat, touching the ground, and spitting in his shirt. He talks to a doctor a few times a month and takes medication every day. I think it's helping. He isn't spitting in his shirt as much as he used to.

I'm thankful my mom and stepdad are more worried about Alex's habits than my fight with Olivia tonight. I don't feel like talking about it anymore because I'm worried about Alex's habits too.

Even though he's two years older, Alex has always been nice to me. We have a lot in common and get along most of the time — except for when he says he's faster or stronger than me. We also don't get along when he's being disrespectful to my mom when his dad is out of town. We spent the afternoon playing Roblox on our iPads and watching rap music videos. Alex says rap is the greatest music ever made and spends a lot of time beatboxing. My mom and stepdad like rap music but wish Alex would try out something new. They're tired of the beatboxing but want to be encouraging.

The great thing about my mom and I guess the okay thing about my stepdad is they encourage us to be who we are. My stepdad isn't so bad. I guess I could be nicer to him. I usually just ignore him. I can tell it hurts his feelings but I guess it's kind of the point. I have one dad and his name is Matthew Parker not Ben Bishop.

"Girls, are you ready for the spelling test tomorrow?" Mom asks.

I'm transported back to the dining table. I get lost in the clouds sometimes. Mom says it's called daydreaming. I guess I'm a daydreamer. I sometimes like to daydream I can teleport out of this house and out of this family.

Olivia sinks into her seat in despair. Her brown eyes well up with tears under her long dark bangs. "I hate spelling, it's too hard. It's impossible!"

"Olivia, please stop. It's not impossible," my stepdad said as he reaches for the pepper. "Please put your plate in the dishwasher and head upstairs to study. Jade, please go and study with your sister." Great, he's bossing me

25

around again. He's not my dad. He's only been my stepdad for a few months.

    It had all happened so fast. My mom and Ben dated for a while and then he asked her to marry him. Two months later they bought a big house and it was fun for like a minute. They let us decorate our rooms however we wanted. We even got to choose a new paint color for our walls. Olivia chose purple everything. Purple walls, purple blankets, a purple canopy, and even a small purple chandelier. I painted my room light blue and picked out a white comforter with small gold polka dots. I have a canopy and chandelier too but the canopy is white and the chandelier is made of crystals. Alex didn't paint his walls. He said he liked the white. He put up a few football, soccer, and basketball posters and said he was done decorating.

    The three of us had to start at a new school this year. Having to say goodbye to all our old friends was the worst part about this summer.

Our new house is twenty minutes away from our old neighborhood. My mom said we could still visit our old friends but a twenty-minute drive might as well be to the moon.

"Jade, did you hear him?" Mom rubs her hands over the sides of her neck. "Please don't be disrespectful."

"Sorry, Mom, I'll go do my homework." I push my chair back from the dining table, careful not to bump Chase. He's the best dog in the world. Ever since he was a puppy, he'd sit under the table next to me during dinner in case a piece of food fell to the floor. Chase wags his tail and I pat his head before grabbing my plate and water glass. He was an especially good boy today, eating the carrots I snuck to him from dinner. I'm glad it's his favorite treat because I hate them. Carrots make me gag. Chase follows me as I take my dishes into the kitchen, place them in the dishwasher, and head upstairs.

I grab my spelling words out of my backpack and some extra paper and a pencil, then take a seat at the big wooden desk us kids share in the office and start to write out my words. Writing out my words a few times before the test helps me remember how to spell them. *Tap, tap, tap.* Olivia taps her pencil on the desk.

"Olivia, stop being annoying." I lean forward in my chair across from her and continue to scribble out my spelling words.

"I can't help it, I'm so bored." She throws her head back toward the giant white dry-erase board on the wall behind her. The white board is the best thing in the whole room. We're supposed to use it for homework but most days Olivia and I just draw on it together.

The office is where my stepdad works from home. I don't understand what he does but he travels to other countries like Japan, Korea, and India a lot. Alex told me his dad works for a big tech company. I'm not sure what he does at the tech company, but he brings us cool souvenirs from his trips so I guess whatever he does there has its perks. My mom works with nurses and doctors at a big hospital downtown. She's the boss. She took me to her office once and I got to sit in her chair and pretend to use her computer. I want to be like my mom when I grow up. I want to dress up in sassy clothes and tell people what to do.

 I peek over at Olivia as she stares at the spelling words on her paper. She isn't looking at the words. She's probably daydreaming like me. Spelling is easier for me than it is for Olivia. She says she wants to be a singer or artist when she grows up and doesn't need to know how to spell. She's probably right. I know Olivia is going to be famous someday but for now we both need to get through the fifth grade. Olivia sniffles and wipes her eyes. I'm still mad at her but I also don't like to see her upset.

 "Are you okay?"

"No, I'm angry," she said.

"Because of cheer practice?" I ask.

"Cheer practice and because of Thomas. I hate him, he's so mean." Olivia puts her head down on the table and lets out a big sigh. She's right, Thomas Walker is mean. He's in our class and a bully. A few weeks ago he told me I had caterpillars on my eyebrows so I told him he had floss on his. He picks on everyone but he likes to pick on Olivia the most. He calls her a baby and told the class she hides a pacifier in her backpack. He even pushed her down on the playground today at recess. Olivia does cry a lot but she isn't a baby and she doesn't have a pacifier. She hates when kids tease her about the crying. My mom told me Olivia has big emotions and sometimes we just need a good cry to feel better.

"I'm not a baby." She buries her head in her hands and sobs.

"I know you're not. He's a bully." I hope It's enough to get her to stop crying but the crying gets louder. I ignore it for a while but my ears start to hurt and it's hard to concentrate on my work.

I can't take it anymore. "Stop crying and write your list so we can do something else."

"Jade, stop bossing me around." She rolls her eyes between sniffles and my face starts to feel hot.

"I'm not bossy! Stay in the fifth grade. I don't care!" I grab my paper and pencil and storm out of the office.

I could help her study. I should help her study. When we were best friends, I would help her study. Not today though. Not after she said I was bossy and definitely not after the way she treated me at practice.

# Chapter Four

"Jade, look out!"

*Whack!* I fall forward on the court as the basketball bounces off of me, scraping my knees and the palms of my hands as I smash into the concrete floor. Ouch, this hurts. I blink to try and keep the tears from falling. Don't cry. Don't cry. Don't cry and embarrass yourself in front of the whole class.

"Are you okay?" I glance up to see a hand reaching toward me and recognize the pink and purple friendship bracelets right away. It's Olivia!

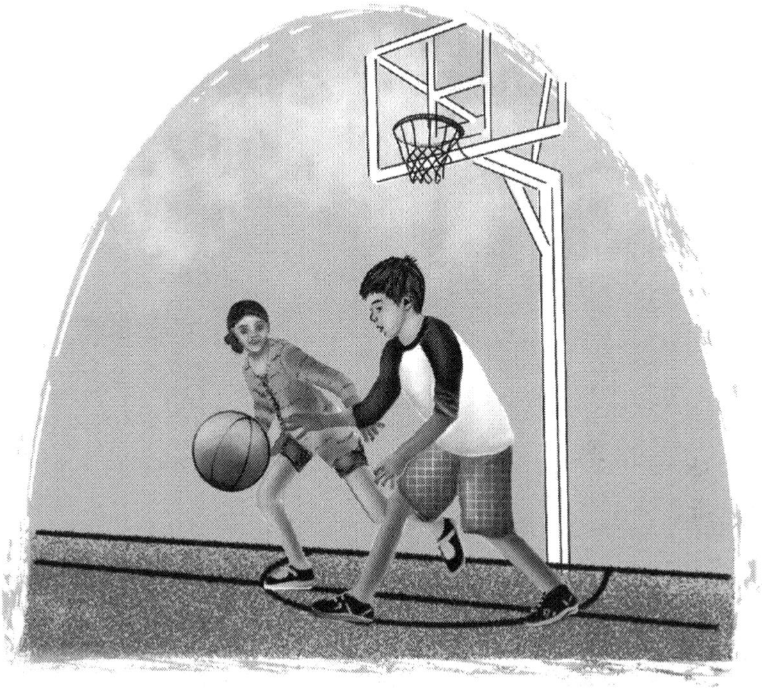

I'm surprised she's still wearing the bracelets my mom made for us. We've been giving each other the silent treatment since last night's fight and it's been more than a little awkward.

The bus ride to school this morning was the worst. Olivia had run ahead of me to sit next to our friend Lilly Callaway. Lilly is in our class and lives one street over. The three of us normally share a seat on the bus but I was still mad at Olivia for what she'd said. There was no way I was going to sit next to her. I had been left with two other options. I could sit next to Thomas or I could sit next to Sam. Sam is a third grader obsessed with the Avengers. Knowing I only had a few seconds to sit down as the bus driver took off, I sat down next to Sam. He talked about the new Avengers movie the entire way to school. It was annoying and put me in a bad mood.

"Are you okay?" Olivia asks again. I had been so shocked it was her, I had forgotten to answer.

"Yeah, I'm okay." I grab her hand and she helps pull me up off the floor as Wyatt Evans rushes over.

"I'm so sorry! It was an accident." He puts his hands on his knees and tries to catch his breath.

"It's okay, Wyatt." I start to dust myself off and pretend like I'm not in pain.

"Your knee is bleeding," Olivia says. "We have to get you a Band-Aid." I look down and see a small drop of blood rolling down my right knee.

Why is she being so nice to me? I'm so confused. We walk in silence to the first-aid kit on the grass next to the fifth grade teachers. There are three fifth grade classes at Hillside Elementary, and they all have lunch and recess at the same time. Recess is twice a day and the highlight of most school days. The teachers like to stand between the play structure and the basketball court during recess. It's the best spot for them to be able to talk and make sure none of the kids are getting into trouble. It's hard to have fun sometimes, knowing they're watching, but today I'm grateful for them and their first-aid kit.

"Mrs. Lane, can we please have a Band-Aid?"

"Of course, here you go." Our teacher, Mrs. Lane, reaches down into a large red box and pulls out a bright neon green Band-Aid. She hands it to Olivia.

"Do you need any help?"
"No, I got it. Thank you," Olivia said as she tears open the Band-Aid and sits on the ground in front of me. Olivia places the Band-Aid over my scraped knee.

"Thank you. Thanks for being so nice," I said.

"We're sisters." Did I hit my head when I fell? Did Olivia just say we're sisters?

"I mean we're stepsisters." She turns and runs back to join Isabel Sutton and Jessica Cohen on the swing set. She jumps on the empty swing next to Jessica and the three of them laugh at something Isabel said. I miss when Olivia was my best friend. Maybe she misses me too? I can't help but feel jealous Jessica is hanging out with Olivia. Jessica was my friend first. Our moms are best friends and we practically grew up together. Being at the same school with Jessica had been one of the few benefits of transferring to Hillside Elementary.

I hurry back to the basketball court where I had been trying to shoot baskets with Wyatt, Lilly, and Caleb before I'd been hit by the ball. My hands are still burning so I watch from the edge of the court. Lilly passes the ball to Wyatt and walks over to join me.

"So weird," Lilly whispers. "I thought you and Olivia weren't friends anymore?"

I'm not really sure what we are, but I say, "I think we're friends but we aren't sisters."

"What?" Lilly sits on the ground and gives me a confused look as she randomly picks at the grass next to the court. "Aren't your parents married?"

Sitting down next to her in the grass, I say, "They're married, but we're stepsisters. We aren't real sisters." I'm starting to get annoyed with her questions.

"Oh, I thought it was the same thing?" Lilly plucks a dandelion out of the ground and sticks it behind her ear. She looks back up at me and then leans over to grab some more grass, the dandelion disappears in her blond hair.

"It's not the same thing." I pluck a handful of grass out of the dirt and throw it up in the air. The blades of grass float back to the ground. I don't want to admit it doesn't make much sense to me either, so I change the subject. "Why is Jessica spending so much time with Olivia? She's supposed to be on my side."

Lilly looks over to the swings and thinks for a minute. "Jessica sat with you during lunch today. I think she's on your side."

It doesn't seem like it right now. I cross my arms and glare over at Olivia and Jessica. "So then why is she swinging with Olivia?" I'm hurt Jessica isn't being a loyal friend.

"I don't know but I hope you and Olivia make up soon. I miss when we all used to hang out together."

The recess bell rings and we run to line up by the doors so we can go back inside and take our spelling test. I miss when we all used to hang out together too.

# Chapter Five

I slam my notebook shut and race to my locker to grab my jacket and backpack. The last bell of the school day has rung, and I fling my backpack over one shoulder and line up behind Mrs. Lane by the classroom door. I don't want to be stuck sitting next to Sam again on the bus. I peek over my shoulder at Caleb standing behind me to see if he notices how loud my heart is pounding in my chest, but he's busy stuffing his sweater into his backpack and doesn't seem to hear. I turn forward and watch Mrs. Lane. Does she hear it?

*Thump, thump, thump.* I feel like my heart is going to explode out of my black hoodie.

"All right, kids, no running in the halls." Mrs. Lane opens the door and leads us outside.

Once we are outside, I run to the line already forming for Bus 16. Success! I'm fourth in line. I sit down at an empty seat toward the middle of the bus and glance out the window to see Olivia waiting to get on. Standing in line a few kids behind her is Lilly. I wonder if Olivia will sit next to me? I wonder if she wants to be friends again? Either way I hope Lilly will sit by me and I won't be stuck sitting next to Sam again.

"Move your backpack." I turn from the window to see who the voice belongs to.

My heart drops into my shoes. It's not Sam. The voice belongs to someone much worse. Thomas. He plops down next to me before I get the chance to tell him the seat is saved. Avoiding eye contact, I scoot my backpack over with my left foot and slink down a little.

I hear Olivia's laughter. I sink lower into my seat and hope she takes an empty seat at the front of the bus. I hope she doesn't see who I'm sitting next to. No such luck. Olivia's face comes into view, and I watch as her smile vanishes. She's spotted me. She picks up her pace and rushes past Thomas and me to the back of the bus.

"What's up with your sister?" I stare out the window and pretend I don't hear him.

"Hello." Thomas waves his hand in front of my face when I don't answer. "What's up with you?" He isn't going to let this go.

"Nothing." I move closer to the window and continue to avoid eye contact.

"You're both ignoring me."
Before I can stop myself, I'm facing him. "Well, yeah, you pushed her at recess."

Thomas rolls his eyes. "So what. I pushed Olivia, not you."

"She's my sister!" My jaw clenches and my ears begin to burn.

Thomas startles and shifts away from me. "Sorry." His eyes narrow and I can tell he's not sorry.

We pull up to my stop and Thomas doesn't get the chance to say anything else. I wait for Olivia at the bottom of the bus steps. I have to tell her I didn't want to sit next to Thomas. He sat next to me! Olivia doesn't stop at the bottom of the steps. Tears stream down her face as she runs past me down the street to our house.

"Olivia, wait!" I try to catch up but she has a head start. She beats me to the house, enters in the door code, and runs up the stairs to her bedroom.

When I knock on her door, she says, "Go away, Jade, I don't want to talk to you!"

43

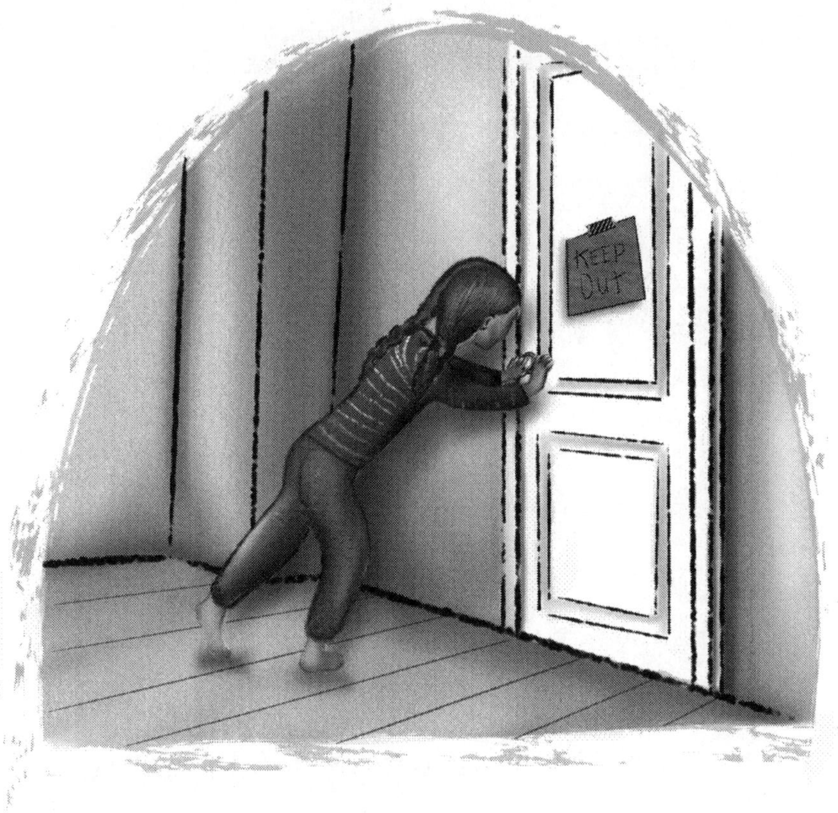
KEEP
OUT

I rest my forehead on her closed bedroom door and try knocking again. "Olivia, am I invited? Can I please talk to you?"

I hold my breath, hoping she'll let me in this time. Being invited before you enter someone's room is one of my favorite house rules. It gives me my space when I want to be left alone. It also keeps pesky older brothers out when Olivia and I are painting our nails and talking about our crushes.

"I said go away!"

I hesitate to leave but I back away from the door. She's too upset. Now is not the best time to talk to her. If Olivia is going to ignore me, I can ignore her too.

At dinner, Olivia is quiet. It's unusual and awkward. I talk a lot but Olivia talks even more than I do. Mom and Ben are usually thankful when we take a break from all the talking but I can tell the war between Olivia and me is starting to stress them out. They want everyone to get along. Mom and Ben look back and forth at each other for a while without saying anything. Halfway through dinner, it's clear they can't take the silence anymore. They attempt to get Olivia and me to talk to each other but neither of us wants to give in.

They ask about our day at school.

"It was fine," Olivia says.

"It was good."

They ask about our homework.

"I finished it." I smile at my mom. She's always proud of me when I get my homework done without her having to ask.

"I'm not done yet." Olivia doesn't look up from her dinner plate.

They ask us if we're excited for the cheer competition next week.

"Yes," we both answer at the same time. No matter what they asked, Olivia and I answered with quick and short responses.

My mom looks at me from across the table and raises her eyebrows toward Olivia. She's motioning for me to say something to her. This is my opportunity. After a few minutes of silence, I finally work up the nerve. "My favorite part of the cheer performance is the last tumbling pass. What's your favorite part, Olivia?"

Olivia continues to look down at her plate. She stuffs a big bite of rice in her mouth to avoid answering me.

"Olivia, please answer Jade." Ben looks over at Olivia and waits for her to acknowledge me but she doesn't.

"I'm full, can I be done?" she asks. Ben lets out a deep breath. "Not until you answer your sister."

"She's not my sister." She slams her spoon down on the table. I feel like a knife twists into my heart. She can't possibly mean that. I'm sure she's just saying things she doesn't mean because she is upset.

"Olivia, that is not okay." Ben's jaw tightens. "Jade is your sister and you will respect our things and our home."

"Please go up to your room," mom said. "You're not my mom, you can't tell me what to do!" Mom sinks back in her chair and I cringe. Olivia's remarks to my mom sound familiar. I'm not much nicer to Ben.

Ben stands up from his chair and leans over the table. "Sophie is my wife. She is also your stepmother. You will respect her. Apologize." His voice is steady and calm but I can tell he's angry by how slow he's talking.

"Fine. I'm sorry. Now can I be done?" Olivia gets up from her seat. She crosses her arms and glares at Ben.

Ben inhales sharply, "Yes, go up to your room." Olivia grabs her plate and rushes out of the dining room. She drops her silverware on the way out.

"Hey, you dropped something." Alex yells after her but she doesn't come back to pick up her spoon and fork.

Alex reaches down and grabs the spoon but before he can grab the fork, Chase swoops in from under the table and grabs the fork in his mouth. I lean to my left and see him race through the dog door in the kitchen. Chase runs to a patch of dirt in the backyard and starts digging a hole to bury the fork. My mom, Ben, Alex, and I laugh as we watch him through the dining room window. For a moment I forget all about my problems with Olivia. Alex jumps up from the table and goes out the back door to retrieve the fork from Chase.

"Alright, dinner's over." Mom starts to clear the table and I'm reminded of my problems with Olivia again. I catch up to Olivia at the top of the stairs.

"Hey are you ok?" I place my hand on Olivia's arm.

Olivia pulls her arm away, "Leave me alone, Jade. I don't want to talk to you about it."

My forehead wrinkles in surprise, "Why not? We're sisters."

"You're not my real sister, Jade!" Olivia runs to her room and closes the door. Silence fills the hallway.

"Well, I hate you and I hate this family!" I slam my bedroom door so hard my dream catcher falls from my light blue wall. There is no way I'm going to let her win this war. War; I'm not even sure how it started. But one thing was certain, I wasn't about to lose to Olivia Bishop, even if she is my stepsister.

# Chapter Six

The next day on the bus to school, I fill Lilly in on everything. "After she said I wasn't her real sister, I ignored her at bedtime and at breakfast." I nod my head with pride. I'm still hurt Olivia said I'm not her sister. Mostly because I once told her how much I had begged my mom for a sister and I'm surprised she would say something so awful after I told her that.

"How long are you going to ignore her?" Lilly asked.

"Until she apologizes." I'd made up my mind last night before bed and nothing was going to make me budge.

"Won't that be hard? We have our science experiment today and we're all in the same group."

I groan and smack my hand to my forehead. Science is my second favorite subject and I'm not about to let Olivia ruin it for me. Turning to Lilly, I say, "Will you help so I don't have to talk to her?"

"How?" Lilly's eyebrows scrunch as she pauses for a second. "I guess I can jump in and do the talking for you if Olivia tries to talk to you."

"Thanks." The bus pulls up to the school and I'm relieved to have Lilly on my side. As I walk into the classroom and see Olivia laughing with Jessica I get an idea. A slow smile stretches over my face. I'm not going to ignore Olivia. I'm going to get even.

When Mrs. Lane turns on the projector a few hours later to display the science experiment instructions, my hands start to shake and the hair on the back of my neck feels damp. I walk to the back of the room with my science lab book and join Olivia, Lilly, and Isabel. Isabel starts reading the instructions. This week's science lesson is about molecule chains and the experiment has something to do with polymers. The instructions projected on the board state we are supposed to inflate a balloon and poke a wooden skewer through it without popping it.

The project has a lot of steps and my heart sinks when Mrs. Lane mentions she's going to have us demonstrate our experiments in front of the class. She assures us that we have enough supplies at our tables to practice before we present. I look over at Olivia and she's staring at the instructions projected on the wall.

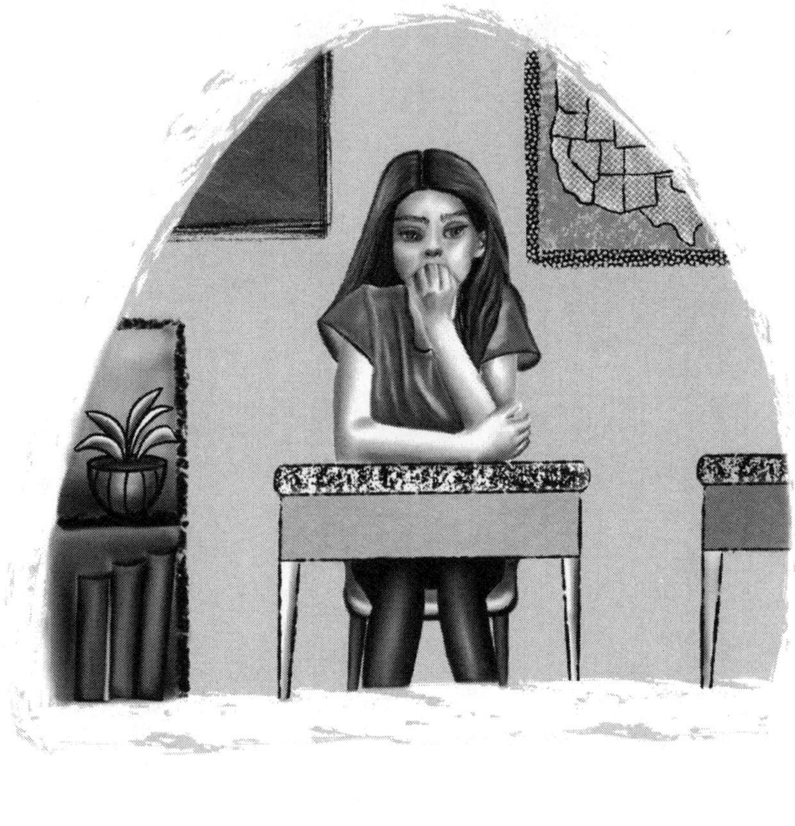

Lilly steps in and suggests we take turns completing the steps. Olivia will go first followed by Lilly, Isabel and then me. Everyone agrees to the plan and Olivia begins step one of the instructions. The final step of the experiment falls to me. My hands are steady. I pick up the skewer Isabel covered in Vaseline in my right hand, then grab the purple balloon Olivia inflated with my left hand. I slowly insert the skewer above where the balloon has been tied. It doesn't pop! Isabel, Olivia, and Lilly cheer. I smile and place the skewered balloon down on the table. I'm confident we're ready to present to the class.

A few minutes later Mrs. Lane calls us all back to our seats and asks the first group to come to the head of the class to perform the experiment. I lean forward in my seat to get a better view. The balloon doesn't pop! The class claps and Mrs. Lane calls my group up next. My heart races as Olivia walks next to me towards the front of the classroom.

This is my chance. I slide my leg over in front of her feet and Olivia goes stumbling onto the ground. Her shoulder slams into Wyatt's desk on the way down. A wave of embarrassment washes over me and concern; embarrassment for what I just did and concern if Olivia is ok. Wyatt reaches down to help Olivia up and as she stands her eyes catch mine and they're brimmed with tears. "You tripped me on purpose!"

I shrug my shoulders, "No I didn't, it was an accident."

"Olivia are you alright?" I break Olivia's icy stare and see Mrs. Lane at our side.

"I'm ok," Olivia says but her face is red and I can tell I've embarrassed her. I stand up at the front of the room and wonder if everyone thinks I did it on purpose. Jessica will never want to be my friend again now but what's worse is I may have lost my sister for good. Isabel hands me the inflated balloon and my hands are shaking. I steady myself as best I can and manage to push the skewer through the balloon without popping it.

"Well done, girls, you've passed today's assignment," Mrs. Lane says as she checks our names off her clipboard. Once the final team conducts their experiment, Mrs. Lane asks us to clean up the supplies and line up for recess.

"Did you trip Olivia on purpose?" Lilly asks as she walks with me to the trash to throw away the balloon.

"Of course, not. I would never do something like that." My stomach sinks again. Tripping Olivia is exactly what I did and now I've lied to one of my best friends. I should have stuck to my original plan of simply ignoring her. I don't think I have the stomach for revenge.

The first recess bell rings and I grab my jacket from my locker and line up behind Jessica. "Let's be on the same basketball team today," I tell her as I slip on my jacket.

"Not today, I promised Olivia I would go on the swings with her," Jessica says. My face turns red but Jessica doesn't turn around to look at me. I knew it! She thinks I tripped Olivia on purpose. I hope no one else heard that she doesn't want to play with me. I look around but everyone seems distracted, putting on their coats and chatting about what they are going to do at recess. They don't seem to notice my embarrassment. I have to find someone to play with and quick before anyone notices.

Once we're outside, I run up to Wyatt and ask if he wants to play basketball. When he agrees, I breathe a sigh of relief and run to the equipment shelf for a basketball. It isn't long before we have enough kids to break out in two teams and start a game but I'm distracted. I'm not playing my best. I keep looking over at the swings where Olivia and Jessica are laughing and swinging like they're new best friends.

"Jade, hello? Are you there?" Wyatt says as I miss another rebound.

"Sorry," I look around in desperation for an excuse, "my shoe keeps coming untied, it's distracting me."

I step out of the game to tie my shoe and look over to the swings again but they're empty. I scan the playground and see Olivia and Jessica standing by the play structure. I watch as Olivia leans toward Jessica. She cups her hand in front of Jessica's ear and whispers something to her. Jessica laughs as Olivia steps away and the two of them turn and look right at me. I can't believe it! Olivia is making fun of me. I would never do something so mean to her. My stomach feels hollow and my body burns hot. I finish pretending to tie my shoe and run to join the basketball game, flashing the biggest fake smile I can. There's no way I'm going to let anyone see me upset.

At lunch, I save a seat for Jessica like I do every day, but she sits down the table with Olivia instead. I start to panic I'll have to eat lunch alone, but Lilly sits down next to me.

"She's ignoring me," I say as I open up my lunch box and pull out my turkey and cheese sandwich. Lilly stops chewing and, with a mouthful of food, asks me who I'm talking about.

"Jessica. Olivia has turned her against me. They were talking about me and laughing behind my back."

Lilly chokes and starts coughing. She takes a sip of juice, then looks at me with wide eyes. "Are you sure? What did they say?"

"I don't know but they looked at me and laughed." My eyes burn as I blink the tears away. I'm not going to cry in front of everyone.

Lilly leans in and gives me a hug. "I'm sorry. Maybe everything will be fine at second recess." I hope she's right.

After lunch Mrs. Lane reads us the next chapter of a book I don't remember. I'm still too distracted thinking about Jessica and Olivia laughing at me.

At second recess, I look for Jessica, but she runs right past me without a word and jumps on a swing next to Olivia. Lilly was wrong. Everything is not fine. Jessica is ignoring me and it's all because Olivia turned her against me. How could she be so mean?

# Chapter Seven

I shuffle my feet across the hard-wood floors in the kitchen and fling open the pantry door. Grabbing a jar of Nutella, I kick the pantry door closed, then grab a spoon out of the silverware drawer. I slam the drawer closed and the silverware rattles.

"Everything okay?" I turn and burst into tears at the sound of my mom's voice.

"Do you want to talk about it?" I nod and place the Nutella and spoon down on the kitchen counter. I wipe the tears from my face with the back of my sleeve and Mom pulls me in for a hug.

We walk into the living room and I throw myself on the couch, wanting to disappear. Shutting my eyes as tight as I can, I bury my face into the dark gray cushions. I hope when I open my eyes, I wake up and it's all been a bad dream. The cushions feel cool against my skin. I'm so warm I wonder if I have a fever. I open my eyes and watch as my mom places a cup of hot chocolate and a cup of tea on the coffee table in front of us. It wasn't a dream. I don't know how long I've been crying but my face is stiff from the dried tears on my cheeks. Hot chocolate always makes me feel better so I sit up and take a few careful sips.

"Do you feel like you're ready to talk now?" Mom asks as I set the empty cup on the table.

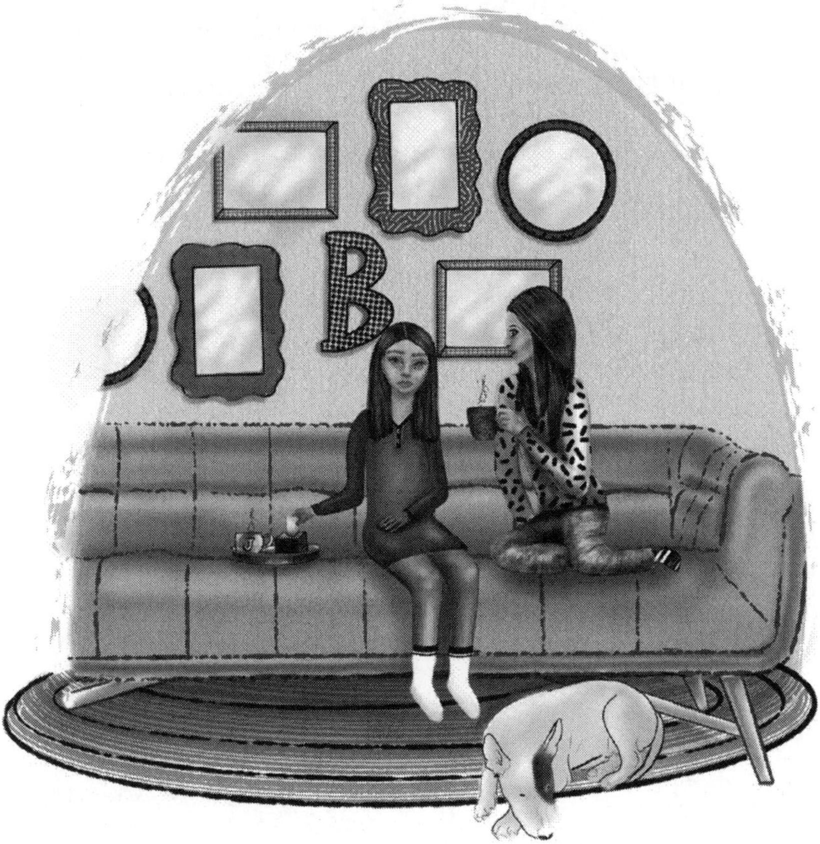

I feel like a boulder is crushing my chest. "Olivia thinks I betrayed her but I didn't." The whole story comes spilling out. "It wasn't my fault. I didn't sit by Thomas. I sat by Sam and I had to listen to the Avengers and it was so annoying. But then Thomas sat next to me and Olivia saw and now she's mad but I didn't do anything. I would never betray her. She betrayed me! She turned my longest friend against me. She's my sister and I love her but now she's mad at me and my whole life is ruined." My chest feels lighter and I feel like I can breathe again.

"Slow down." My mom grabs my hands with hers and kisses me on the forehead. "I'm confused, I thought you didn't sit by Thomas?"

"I didn't sit by him yesterday on the way to school, but he sat by me on the way home."

"Is sitting next to Thomas a bad thing?" she asks.

"Yes, he pushed Olivia at recess and is Olivia's worst enemy." Did my mom not hear anything I said?

"Pushing Olivia wasn't a very nice thing to do. Did you tell Mrs. Lane?" Mom's eyebrows are raised and I can sense her concern.

I hesitate to respond. I know my mom is going to be disappointed. "No. I'm sorry, Mom, I forgot."

She squeezes my hand reassuringly. "It's okay, but next time please tell her so she can help you."

I gaze down at the floor. "I know, Mom. I should tell the teacher if someone is being a bully."

"Yes, but either way, it sounds like this is all a misunderstanding. I'm sure Olivia will understand what happened once she calms down and you get a chance to talk to her." Mom lets go of my hands and moves a few strands of damp hair off my face. "What's all this about not being friends with Jessica and Olivia turning her against you?"

"Jessica used to be my best friend but now she's Olivia's best friend." I wipe my eyes and look up at my mom.

"Did she say she wasn't your friend anymore?" Mom asks. "Is she ignoring you?"

"She didn't say she doesn't want to be friends but she acts like it. Her and Olivia were whispering about me today. She doesn't spend time with me anymore. She just wants to go on the swings with Olivia." I sniffle a few times and wipe my nose with the back of my hand.

Mom hands me a tissue and I wipe my nose. "Are you sure they were whispering about you? Did they say you can't join them?"

"They looked right at me and laughed! They invite me to swing sometimes but I don't want to. I want to play basketball." I hand the tissue back to my mom. "Jessica used to always play basketball with me. I bet Olivia said bad things about me and now Jessica doesn't want to be my friend anymore."

"I don't know," Mom says. "It sounds like you're assuming a lot about Jessica and about Olivia. They could have been talking about something else. I really think you should talk to Jessica. This doesn't sound like her at all. It sounds like she still wants to be your friend and just wants to do something else at recess."

"I'm scared to talk to her. What if she says she doesn't want to be my friend anymore?" I fidget with the edge of the couch cushion.

"That happens sometimes with friends. We can't force people to want to be around us. There will always be someone who doesn't like you. Do you like everyone?" Mom asks as she leans in closer to me.

I cross my arms. "No, I don't like Thomas."

"What if I said you had to hang out with him?"

"I would be angry. I don't want to be around him."

"Okay, so would it be okay if someone doesn't like you or doesn't want to spend time with you?" Mom asks.

I hesitate to give her an answer. I want everyone to like me. "I guess so."

"Focus on spending time with the people who like you and love you, not the ones who don't. You'll drive yourself crazy otherwise. I really do think Jessica is still your friend but if she doesn't want to be friends anymore, you can spend time with Lilly or Wyatt or Isabel. You're also still so new at school. This might be a good chance to get to know some of the other kids in your class a little better." I'm reluctant but nod in agreement.

"You also have a sister and a brother who love you," Mom says.

I can feel my eyes start to burn again and I blink quickly to stop myself from crying. "I don't think Olivia loves me anymore. She said I'm bossy and we're not real sisters." I take a deep breath before I tell her the really bad part, "Also, I might have tripped her on purpose during science."

I pick at the black nail polish on my fingers as she opens and closes her mouth, obviously not knowing what to say. Chase wakes up from his nap by the fireplace, comes over, and rests his head on my lap. His presence calms me, and I pet his head in thanks.

After taking a deep breath, Mom starts speaking again. "I'm disappointed that you would retaliate like that. You know that's never the answer. Did you apologize?"

I shake my head no with regret, "Not yet, but I'm going to. I feel really bad about it."

Mom nods her head, "Good, you should try to apologize as soon as you can. It really wasn't the right thing to do."

I wipe a tear off my cheek, "Do you think Olivia doesn't love me anymore?"

"I'm sure she still loves you. I don't think Olivia meant it when she said you're not her sister. Her mom says a lot of mean things about us. She thinks we're different. It puts Olivia in a tough position because she loves her mom." She takes a sip of her tea. "Olivia loves us too. She's a sweet girl but it's confusing for her."

"We're not different. Can you tell Olivia's mom to stop being so mean?" When Olivia and I were friends, she told me her mom Kimberly had a lot of problems. Kimberly had been taken away from her family when she was a baby and had no memory of them. The only connection she had to her birth family was her last name, Mite. Kimberly bounced around in different houses with different people until she was old enough to get an apartment on her own. She works a lot so Olivia and Alex are usually with babysitters when they're at their moms. On the rare days when she isn't at work, her mom has a hard time getting out of bed. She lets Olivia and Alex watch tv all day. Olivia said her mom cries every night after she thinks they're asleep, but Olivia can hear her through the bedroom wall. My stepdad and mom worry a lot about Olivia and Alex when they aren't with us.

"I'd rather not talk to Kimberly, and even if I did, I don't think it would make a difference. We can't control other people and what they say or do. We can only control how we react." Mom places her cup on the table and pulls me in for a hug.

"Some people only feel comfortable around people who look and act like they do. I think they're missing out. Being Persian is a part of who you are. It makes you unique. I think it would be boring if everyone was the same." I nod and try to absorb everything my mom is saying. I like my dark hair, big eyes, and long black eyelashes. I wish Olivia's dad had married my mom first so we wouldn't have to deal with mean Kimberly.

"I know once Olivia calms down and you talk to her, everything will be okay."

"Okay, Mom. I'll try again after dinner."

"Great. I'll let you know when dinner's ready." She gives me one last hug and walks out of the room as I start looking for something to watch on tv.

I just hope she's right.

# Chapter Eight

After another quiet dinner, I head up to my room and settle under my covers with a book from my favorite mystery series. I'll talk to Olivia at bedtime. Right now, I need some space and time to myself. I get lost in the words and before I know it, Mom's calling us to get ready for bed. I slip on my pajamas and I'm the first one in the bathroom to brush my teeth. Alex and Olivia are standing outside the bathroom door waiting their turn.

"Goodnight, Jade," Alex says as Olivia rushes past me in the doorway and shuts and locks the bathroom door.

"Goodnight, Alex." I'll have to wait until she's out of the bathroom to talk to her.

I head downstairs to tell my mom goodnight and when I get back upstairs, Olivia's bedroom door is closed and the lights in the bathroom and hallway have been turned off. I take a deep breath and knock on her door but she doesn't answer. I knock again, a little louder this time and wait for a response but there is none. With a sigh, I back away from the door and head to my room. I guess talking to her will have to wait until tomorrow.

In the morning Olivia is up and out the door and on the bus before me. She sits next to Sam on a seat behind the bus driver and I sit next to Lilly a few rows back. I try to catch up to her on the way to the classroom but I get stuck behind the crowd. She's already at her desk when

I walk into the room. I place my backpack and jacket in my locker and take a seat across the room at my desk. I'll have to talk to her at recess.

"Good morning, kids. Please take out your math workbooks and let's get started." Mrs. Lane works through a few fraction problems on the chalkboard and instructs us to turn to page seventeen in our workbooks.

I've always loved school, and math is my favorite subject. I work through the fraction problems with ease and move on to page eighteen. History and a short writing assignment follow the math lesson. The bell rings and I place my writing notebook inside my desk and grab my jacket to line up for recess. This is my chance. I have to talk to Olivia and I have to talk to Jessica. I slip on my jacket as I walk to the line and pass by Jessica's locker. Jessica is still there struggling to zip up her raincoat. Talking to her will be easier than talking to Olivia, so I decide to go for it.

"Hey Jessica, can we talk at recess?"

"Sure, what do you want to talk about?" she asks as she untangles the thread stuck in her coat zipper.

"Girls, please line up." Mrs. Lane turns out the classroom light and leads the class out of the room. Jessica and I line up behind Wyatt and follow the class to the playground. We walk down the long hallway in silence as Jessica zips up her raincoat and throws the hood over her head. The words spill out as soon as we step outside.

"Do you not want to be friends anymore?" I ask as we walk over to the covered portion of the playground. I drag my boots back and forth through the mud as we walk.

"What are you talking about?" Jessica turns toward me and raises her eyebrows. "You're one of my best friends."

I let out the breath I was holding. "I am? Then why were you and Olivia talking about me and laughing about me at recess yesterday?"

Jessica's eyes widen. "Talking about you? We didn't talk about you, I promise." Jessica scrunches her eyebrows for a moment and then her face relaxes into a smile and she starts laughing.

"Hey, it's not funny!" I cross my arms and glare at her.

"We weren't laughing at you. We were laughing at Caleb. He was making faces at Mrs. Lane behind her back. Olivia was whispering so he wouldn't get caught and so we wouldn't get in trouble for laughing about it."

I picture Caleb making faces at Mrs. Lane and laugh. "Okay, so then why don't you hang out with me at recess anymore?"

Jessica shrugs her shoulders. "I hang out with you sometimes. I'm just tired of basketball. Swinging is more fun. Do you want to swing with us?" she asks.

My stomach sinks into my shoes, "Olivia's mad at me, she won't want me to join."

"I'm not mad at you though. I miss playing with you at recess." She grabs my hand and pulls me toward the swings. "Come on, let's go."

"Okay." I follow her to the swing set. "Can we take turns picking what we do though? I get bored swinging sometimes."

"Sure, how about we swing at first recess and then play basketball at second recess?" Jessica asks.

A big smile stretches over my face. "Perfect!" We run off to the swings and I'm starting to feel better than I have in days. I jump on the swing next to Jessica and look over to Olivia, who is swinging a few kids down. I stretch my legs out toward the sky and then back toward the ground as I propel higher and higher. I can talk to Olivia at second recess. The sun peeks through the clouds and I squint my eyes.

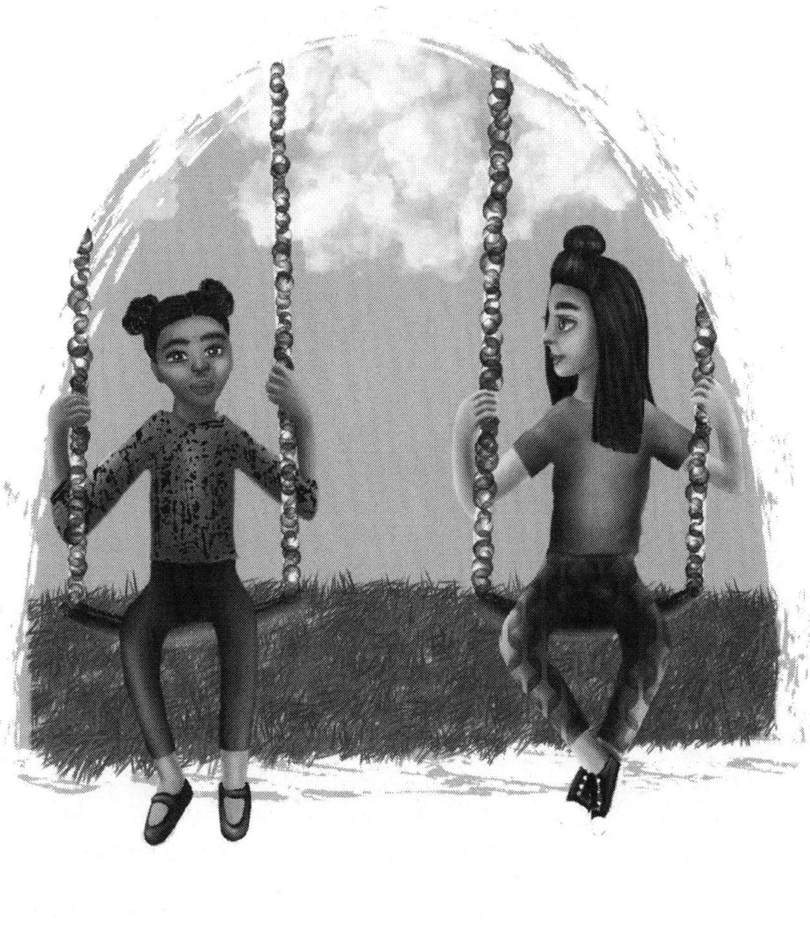

When the bell rings, I jump off the swing and run to line up for lunch. After lunch, we cut construction paper into the shape of turkeys for art class. When the last glue stick is put back, and all of the paper is cleaned up, Mrs. Lane reads us a story about Pilgrims and Native Americans and then it's off for second recess.

"Jade, your shot." Wyatt throws me the basketball as I step out onto the playground. I watch as Olivia runs to the swings with Isabel.

"Okay, but just for a little bit." I can catch up to Olivia on the swings in a minute.

I dribble the ball toward the hoop and aim. The ball goes through the net and Jessica runs up and gives me a high five. Caleb and a few of the other fifth grade boys join and we break out into teams and start playing. I realize I've lost track of time when the bell rings. I've lost my chance to talk to Olivia. I walk toward the school building with the rest of the fifth graders. I can talk to Olivia after school at cheer practice.

# Chapter Nine

It's another uncomfortable bus ride home. I grab an empty seat behind the bus driver and Lilly sits down next to me. A few minutes later, Olivia boards the bus and sits next to Lilly. The three of us share a seat and pretend like Olivia and I aren't fighting, but we're doing a terrible job pretending. There's nothing normal about the bus ride home. Instead of the usual laughter and inside jokes between the three of us, Olivia and I have separate conversations with Lilly. We avoid eye contact and we avoid speaking to each other. When we reach the house from the bus stop, my hair is dripping and my clothes are soaked from the rain. Mom is home early and greets us by the door.

"Hi, pretty girls! Cheer practice was canceled today, so why don't you go change and I'll make you a snack."

"Hi. Why was cheer practice cancelled?" I ask as I take off my wet jacket and shoes and place them in the hall closet.

"There was a leak in the gym but they're working on getting it fixed today. They re-scheduled practice to tomorrow."

"Okay. I hope we have practice tomorrow. We really need to work out the problems with landing the basket toss." I run up the stairs, but when I hear Olivia and my mom talking downstairs, I slow down and lean over the banister to hear them. I peek over the side of the railing so I can see Olivia and my mom below me.

"Sophie, will I see dad before I go to my mom's tomorrow?"

"Yes, he'll be back tomorrow morning." Mom's shoulders relax and her eyes soften. My stepdad's been in San Francisco since yesterday and Alex has been difficult since he left. He doesn't always listen to my mom when his dad is gone. She tries to be patient with him and act like it doesn't bother her. It makes me angry and it makes Olivia sad. I stick up for my mom and then Alex gets mad at me. It usually starts a fight and stresses my mom out even more. Olivia apologizes to my mom a lot when Alex is being mean. It's not Olivia's fault or my mom's fault. I'm starting to feel like having my stepdad around isn't so bad after all. He's good at managing things between my mom and Alex. I hate to admit it but I'm starting to like when he is around.

"Great!" Olivia's tone picks up and I rush to the bathroom to brush my matted wet hair as she skips past me into her room.

My stomach growls as I change my clothes. I go into the kitchen and take a seat at the kitchen island where my mom has put out string cheese and apple slices. As I take a piece of cheese, I peer over my shoulder and look out the window. It's dark already. My body stiffens. I hate November. I jump up and turn on the back-porch light. The branches of the trees in the backyard sway in the wind. The rain taps on the windows and side of the house. The sound is creeping me out. My mom and Olivia are both upstairs. Alex took off for his friend Diego Martinez's house when he got home from school. Diego lives a few streets over and Alex usually heads over there a few times a week to play video games.

"Hey, Alexa, play Selena Gomez." Music flows through the kitchen. My voice steadies and my hands stop trembling as I sing along in between bites of string cheese. Olivia walks into the room and joins me at the kitchen island. She pretends she doesn't see me and starts singing.

"Girls, we need to pick up Alex. He's late and he's not answering his phone." Olivia and I clean up our snack and walk toward the front of the house where mom sits at the bottom of the staircase and slips on her brown leather boots. Mom grabs her jacket from the coat rack and slips her left arm through the sleeve.

I start to ask if we can stay home but Olivia beats me to it. "Can we please stay here? We promise to be good."

My mom pauses and then slips her right arm through the coat sleeve. They never leave us home alone. "Come on, girls, it'll be quick. It's starting to get late."

This is my opportunity. She's wavering. "It's just a few minutes, Mom, please."

"Okay, I'll be right back. I'll set the alarm." She gives me a quick kiss, says "Start on your piano homework," and rushes out the door. Olivia flashes me a quick smile and we run up to our bedrooms to continue ignoring each other.

I grab my lesson book off the floor in my bedroom and take a seat in front of the keyboard. I flip the pages in the lesson book until I reach my assigned song for the week. I jump at the sound of thunder outside my window. I steady my nerves and start playing. I'm halfway through playing the song when I'm surrounded by darkness.

Olivia screams from her room down the hall. I try to run out of my room but my foot catches on the doorframe and I tumble to the floor. Graceful, I mutter to myself. It takes a few minutes for my eyes to adjust to the darkness. My door, the staircase, and Olivia's door come into focus. If I squint just right, I can make out their

87

shapes long enough to walk to Olivia's room without bumping into anything.

"Olivia, where are you?"

"I'm over here by the bed," she says.

I try to picture where all of Olivia's furniture is. I stretch my arms out in front of me and shuffle my feet across the room until I reach her. Olivia is sitting on the floor in front of the bed, holding a pillow to her chest.

I sit down next to her. "It's okay, I'm sure the power will come back on soon."

"I know, but I hate the dark." Olivia sniffles and clings to the pillow.

I reach out my hand toward Olivia. I hate it too, but knowing Olivia needs me gives me strength. "I promise everything will be okay."

Olivia loosens her grip on the pillow and grasps my right hand with hers.

"Mom will be home soon." Olivia rubs her eyes and sits closer to me. The moon shines through the window and casts our shadows across the floor. This is my chance to apologize for tripping her during science class. I take a deep breath to calm my nerves but Olivia starts talking first.

"I'm sorry I said you're not my real sister." Olivia lowers her head and stares at the ground. "It's not nice and it's not true."

"You hurt my feelings." I know Olivia apologized but I can't shake off my hurt feelings.

"I know but I didn't want to hurt my mom's feelings," Olivia says. "She's so sad and angry all the time. I want her to be happy."

"Your mom's not here, Olivia." I grab the sides of my head and hunch over. "What does she have to do with this?"

"Alex tells her everything. She gets so mad when I say you're my sister. She gets even more mad if I say nice stuff about your mom."

My eyes widen. "Do you talk bad about my mom?"

90

Olivia hugs the pillow tight and takes a deep breath. "Sometimes." She rests her head on top of it. "I'm sorry."

The floor warms my hands as I pinch the carpet threads. "How could you? You're not mean. You're not mean like your mom." I swallow the lump forming in my throat. My mom is so nice to Olivia. She does everything for her. Olivia's mom doesn't even take care of her. How can you love someone when they act so ugly?

"My mom's not mean. You're not being nice," Olivia snaps. "I said I was sorry."

The rain pours over the sides of the gutters outside. My stomach flip-flops and the palms of my hands start to sweat. Olivia's right. I'm being mean to her mom but I can't help the anger I still feel about Olivia saying bad things about her. Before I can stop myself the words come out of my mouth "Your mom sucks. She doesn't even take care of you." My lungs deflate and I know I've made a mistake. I should have just let it go.

Olivia springs to her feet, "I hate you! Get out of my room!"

I slowly make my way out of her room. When I reach the door I turn to face her, "Olivia I'm sorry, I didn't mean it" but she slams the door in my face. I'm careful not to bump into anything as I make my way back to my room. I sit down on my bed and stare out the window into the dark gloomy night.

I defended my mom by putting down Olivia's mom. I'm retaliating, and not retaliating is another house rule. I rest my head in my hands and take a few deep breaths. Olivia loves her mom and I love my mom. I made her feel how I felt: angry and sad to hear someone I love saying bad things about someone else I love. I wasn't being kind. The worst part is I didn't even apologize for tripping her. I needed to make this right.

# Chapter Ten

Dear Olivia,

I'm so sorry I said those awful things about your mom. I didn't mean them. I promise to never do it again. I'm also sorry for tripping you during science class. I was angry and wanted to get even but I made a horrible mistake. I feel terrible about it. I'd really like to be your sister and your friend again. Please forgive me.

−Jade

I slip the letter into Olivia's backpack that night after everyone has gone to bed. She's sure to see it in the morning when she packs up her backpack for school. Chase keeps me company as I toss and turn through the night. I'm anxious to see Olivia's reaction to my letter. Will she still hate me in the morning? Will she ignore me? Will I wake up to find out last night was just a bad dream?

When the buzzer of my alarm clock wakes me in the morning, I grown and bury my head under the covers. I don't think it was a dream. I slowly get dressed and when I step out into the hallway Olivia walks right passed me like she doesn't even see me. Terrified of her response, I avoid eye contact during breakfast. The silence continues all day at school and at cheer practice in the afternoon. Olivia doesn't even say goodbye when Kimberly picks her up after cheer for the weekend. I'm starting to second guess my letter to Olivia. She surely must have seen it by now.

Did I say enough? Did I say too much? My dad picks me up after cheer and I spend the weekend at his house worried about what will happen when we return to school on Monday. Would she forgive me after she's had some time to think about it or would spending the weekend with her mom just make her hate me more?

    My dad drops me off at school a few minutes early on Monday morning in the hopes that I can talk to Olivia before school. I stand and pace outside of the classroom until the first bell rings but Olivia never shows up. I reluctantly go to class. Mrs. Lane works through a math problem on the chalkboard but I'm distracted. I keep turning around to look at Olivia's empty seat, hoping to see that she's there but she doesn't arrive to school until after math class. She waves and smiles at me as she sits down. The anxiety I had felt all weekend and morning leave me as I wave back at her. Maybe my letter had been a good idea after all?

When the bell rings for lunch, I quickly clear my desk and walk over to Olivia. She's placing the last of her papers inside her desk and doesn't see me.

I hesitate to speak but push down the butterflies in my stomach as best I can with a few deep breaths, "Hi Olivia."

Olivia looks up from her desk and her eyes light up, "Hi Jade! Thank you for the note. It meant a lot to me."

The butterflies in my stomach stop fluttering, "I was really worried you wouldn't forgive me. I really am sorry for what I said about your mom. I'm really sorry for tripping you too. I feel really bad about it."

Olivia stands up and reaches her arms around me in a hug, "It's ok. I'm sorry for what I said too. Can we call a truce? I don't want to fight anymore."

"I don't want to fight anymore either," a wave of relief washes over me, "truce." I smile at

Olivia and we join our classmates in line to head to the cafeteria for lunch.

---

"Pump it up, pump it up, keep that Wildcats spirit up!" It's Saturday and the day of the big cheer competition. I watch the Wildcats cheer squad perform their routine and I hate to admit it, but they're good. The confidence I felt when we entered the stadium for the cheer competition is dwindling. They finish their routine with a combination of flips and back handsprings. The crowd cheers as the Wildcats exit the stage.

"Girls, we're up after the break." Coach Meyer gathers our team of twelve girls backstage for some final stretches.

"They were really good," Olivia said. She shakes out her hands and jumps several times in place. She looks nervous.

"I'm nervous too, but we've got this," I tell her as I jump in place next to her. Olivia and I haven't talked about being sisters since the power outage last week. Things have been going so well with us as friends, I don't want to jinx it by asking.

Olivia stops jumping and reaches down to touch her toes. She stands upright and nods her head. "You're right. We have a great routine and we didn't miss any of the steps in rehearsal this morning."

A whistle blows and Coach Meyer signals us to gather around for a quick pep talk before our performance. I join my right hand in the middle of the circle with my other teammates' hands. Everyone is nervous but excited to perform. We've been practicing our stunts for weeks. Olivia and I are both flyers on the team and we had been chosen to perform the most difficult stunt of the performance, side by side double twist basket tosses. It had been a tricky combination to learn. There had been a few misses in the beginning but after countless hours of practice we had perfected it.

"Go Blaze," we cheer as we throw our right hands up in the air.

"Please welcome to the stage Blaze!" The announcer's voice booms over the loudspeakers and my heart races as we take our positions on stage. I look out in the audience and spot my mom sitting next to Ben, Alex, and my dad. They are sitting in the third row. Ben had insisted they arrive early to get good seats. Mom has her phone out ready to capture our routine. I scan the crowd and Kimberly is sitting next to one of the few empty seats toward the back of the stadium.

I take a deep breath and steady my nerves. The music starts and we begin our routine of flips, back handspring, and toe touch jumps. Halfway through our routine, the music stops for the cheer portion. I move into formation with the other members of the cheer squad. I clap my hands and hit my cheer positions as we chant, "B-L-A-Z-E, let me hear it, B-L-A-Z-E, Blaze is here to win it." Olivia and I move forward to prepare for the final stunt of the performance. "We've got the spirit, we've got the fight, we're gonna hit it with all our might."

I'm thrown up in the air and I cross my arms across my chest and twist once, then twice in the air to complete the basket toss. The crowd cheers as I'm placed on the ground. I throw my arms up in a final v motion and the routine is over. I hold my pose as my chest rises and falls with the quick breathes filling my lungs.

The announcer welcomes the next team to perform, "Thank you, Blaze! Next up, please welcome Eclipse!"

We wave as we exit the stage. Olivia runs up to me backstage and gives me a big hug. I smile and we celebrate with the team for a few moments before we have to return to our seats.

There are several more teams before the award ceremony, but I have so much adrenaline pumping through me that I barely take in any of the performances. The wait is unbearable. Once the final team leaves the stage, the judges huddle together to vote on the winner. The head judge walks to the middle of the stage and the crowd quiets.

"I want to thank all of the teams that competed today. You were all wonderful. Let's hear a round of applause for all of the amazing cheer squads we saw today." The crowd claps while I bite my nails and hunch forward in my seat.

"I'd like to call the top three teams to the stage, Mustangs, Spirit…" Please say Blaze, please say Blaze. "…and Blaze!" I turn to Olivia sitting next to me and we both scream and jump from our seats. We run on stage with our teammates and the other two squads. The head judge motions for everyone to quiet down and announces Mustangs as the second-place winners. He hands them their trophy and medals and the crowd quiets down again. If he doesn't call our name next, then the Spirit squad has won and we are the third-place winners.

He lifts the microphone up toward his face and I hold my breath and close my eyes. "The winner is Blaze!" Olivia grabs me by the arms, and we jump up and down and scream along with our team. The judge hands us our medals and our coach waves the trophy up in the air in celebration.

I place my medal around my neck and turn to Olivia. This is my chance, I'm going to be brave. "Can we be sisters again?"

"Real sisters and real best friends," Olivia said as she pulls me in for a hug.

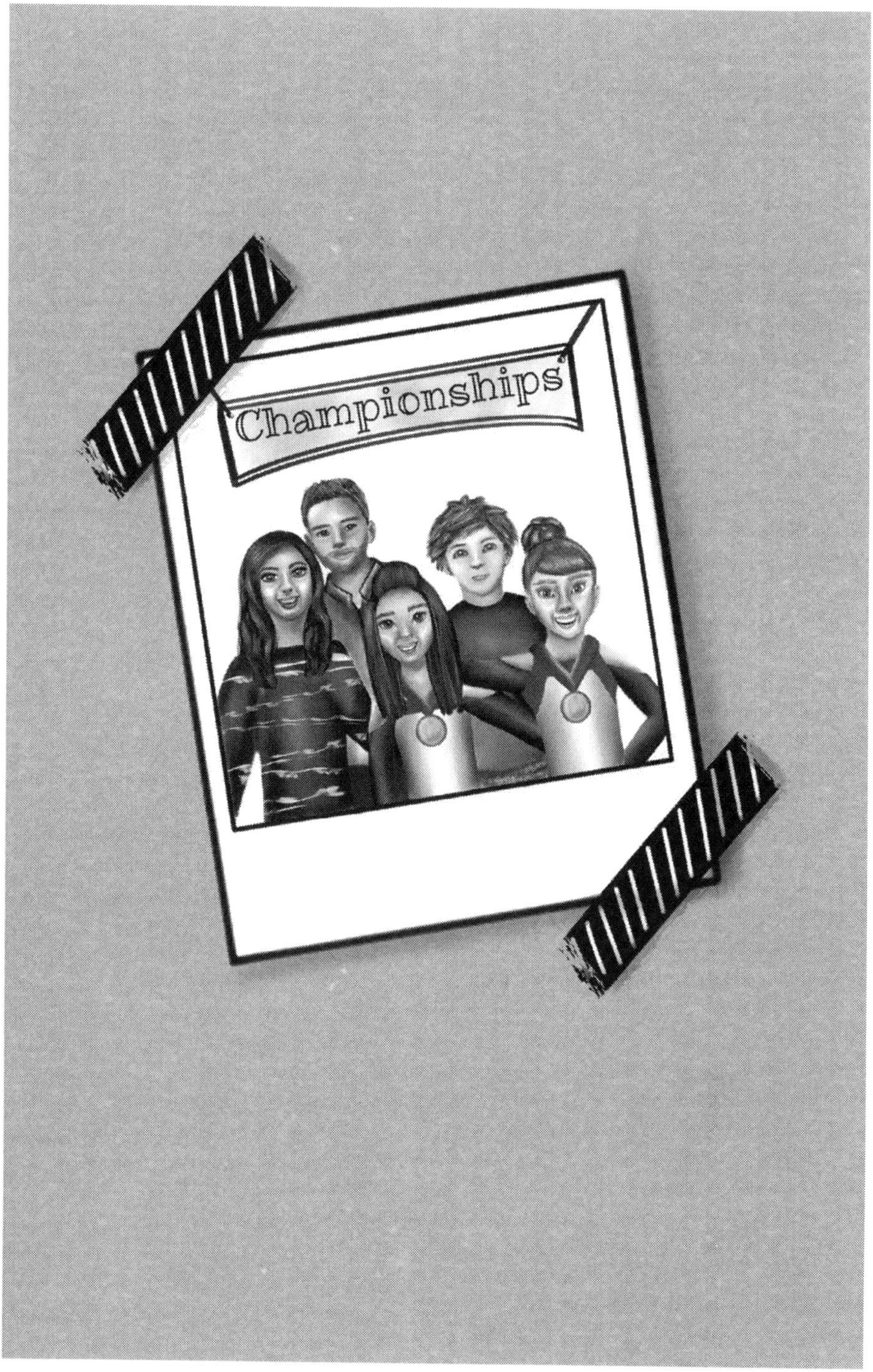
Championships

Made in the USA
Middletown, DE
05 November 2020